BEYOND THE SUNSET

*Collection of Poems mirroring my Life Story
as a Woman and as a Domestic Helper in HongKong
From 2010 to 2021*

by

AILENEMAE RAMOS

She is a simple woman.
A daughter.
A wife.
A mother.
A friend.
A helper.
A fighter.

DEDICATION

I want to dedicate my simple work to all the women, wives, mothers to find love their passion, divert their emotions into something that will boost their self-confidence, and be the best version of themselves.

There are a lot of opportunities out there, it depends on how we create our own story and be the inspiration of the young generations.

Be kind.

Be humble.

Be simple.

Be humane.

Be authentic.

ACKNOWLEDGEMENTS

I sincerely thank Poetry Planet Publishing House for believing and allowing me to publish my writings.

Gratitude is highly given to my family, to all my friends whom I met in person, and virtually, always there to encourage me to love and keep doing my passion for writing.

Thank you so much.

- Ailenemae

Copyright © 2021 BEYOND THE SUNSET
By Ailenemae Ramos
ISBN
978-621-8253-83-4 – hardbound
978-621-8253-85-8 - softbound
978-621-8253-84-1 – mobile/kindle

Published by Poetry Planet Book Publishing House
Edited by Marie Ezekiel
Designed by Tess Ritumalta
Cover photos by Ailenemae Ramos

INTRODUCTION

"Hope" is what I want to emphasize in my "Beyond the Sunset" book. I grew up with hope in my heart that my mother is watching me beyond each sunset. Many times I found myself crying and talking in the dusk as if it was alive and I ask for guidance.

What is Sunset to me? The sunset is just like an end-point. All the burdens and worries deep inside me need to put an end to.

This book is uniquely extraordinary because every word and the phrase I used reflected my emotions as I give life to my imaginations and recap my experiences.

As a dreamer and a fighter, I also love to explore and learn new things. I studied and observed several poetry communities to enlighten my knowledge and improve my writing skills.

It is the reason I was able to create this book....

The Author

PREFACE

The writings emblazoned in this book are based on the life experiences of the author, mirroring her innermost emotions about sadness, anxiety, hope, love, and self-confidence.

Living abroad, where one must adapt to new people, new surroundings, a new language, cultures, food, and traditions, even battling loneliness, challenges, sufferings of being miles and miles away from loved ones, friends, familiar environment and surroundings is never easy.

The Author did find a way to not bottle her emotions while working as an OFW miles away from the ones she loves and cherish.. she entered a world of poetry skillfully painting through words her emotions, and as a daughter longing for her mother in heaven, the yearnings, thoughts, imaginations and ideas, and keeping them safely in a codex she named; "Beyond The Sunset" where anyone wanting to find out for themselves can unlock and discover the world she, Ailenemae, created.

This book is very special as it also highlights the Author's amiable qualities and personalities that can deeply penetrate our souls, creating in us inspirations.

Please enjoy Ailenemae's First Authored poetry book.

Surely, this book is a must-read by women who have a hard time uncovering their self-worth to discover how they can be accepted and feel fulfilled…

The Publisher

TABLE OF CONTENTS

BEYOND THE SUNSET

When I was a child
I used to sit on the ground,
Waiting for the sun setting in the sky
And imagine your face watching over me.

I grew up believing
That in every sunset you were there.
Looking down at me
From Heavens above.

Oh, Mother! I wish you were here.
I missed you so badly.
After each sunset,

I wish you were in my dreams
To feel you hugging me tightly.

I never got a chance to say I LOVE YOU!
To say I'll miss you!
To see you personally!
And even to be loved by you!

Where are you now?
Please let me feel you.
Show yourself even only in my dreams
And let me see you.
I know it cannot happen anymore
No matter how I try.

The sunset is so beautiful, most people adore it.
I always believe that you're there, beyond.
I never missed watching each day of my life.
Praying you'll always there looking after me.

I AM A WOMAN

I am a woman!
I am simple!
I am a strong,
An independent woman.
Let me repeat myself,
as I know,
you weren't listening.
I am a strong,
Independent woman!

I am strong
because I am not afraid
to fall and stumble.
I will fly,
and get my way
through the barriers
to lead to the top of it all
to my destiny.
I will break the chains
of unfairness and mistreatment
that restrains me
from reaching my dreams in life.
I will break free from the cage
of your bitterness.

I may be a woman,
a female but you will no longer
distinguish me.
I am a strong,
Independent woman!

I am a woman!
I dream to have inner peace.
I am a precious gift,
birthed from the womb
of a Goddess.
My heart always
remembers life matters.
My perceptions, feelings,
and thoughts matter.
I won't allow the imperfection
of another soul
to weaken my courage
and make me feel small.
I'll rise above them.
Breathe and relax.
I will open my heart
and see the beauty of who I am.
I will never let the hatefulness
of someone's heart threaten my peace.

I am a woman!
I make my dreams happen!
I have strived hard
on where I am now.
I have sacrificed my uncertainties,
Anxieties and self-limiting beliefs
to be here.
I do celebrate,
and stand firm in my heart.
I won't let the insecurities
of others dragged me down.
I am more than the names
they try to put on me.
I'll rise dearest self.
I'll rise.

I lift the heart to the sky,
see the rainbow as a sign
I have the right to be free
and loved freely –
without fear, shame
or walking on eggshells.
Thinking of all roads I crossed
lead to my heart's awakening,
growth and resilience.
When I feel lost, small in spirit,
isolated and alone.

I know I am concealed,
I am safe, protected, and cared about.

And there you are,
that quiet voice begging me up,
cheering along,
reminding me who I am.
Again and again,
you keep coming around.
You are the small bird
sitting on my window sill,
wishing me well.
You are the wind beneath my wings,
my angel in disguise,
the blood that runs in my veins,
my inner soul,
keep reminding me that I am worthy.

My heart is precious,
I keep my feet rooted in the ground.
And I stood, delighted to myself.
Bowed my head,
lowering my shoulders,
Finding my breath
and look the world in the eye.
Walk away with your head held high.
Away from the pain

and sadness into a lifetime
of absolute truth
that I am alive
and I will get through.
I will make my dreams into reality.
I will live peacefully.
Keep well, dearest self,
I love you.

I am a woman!
I am simple yet stronger than before!
I am firm!
I am bold!
I am unique!
I am extraordinaire!
I am worthy!
And I am fulfilled!

BEING SELFLESS

I am a mother being selfless,
when it comes to my children.

Being a mother,
I will do everything for them.
I will sacrifice anything for them.
I will give comfort and protection to them.
I will think of their welfare before my own.

I do care for them unconditionally.
I do care for them since they were little.
I do care for them on how to love each other.
I do care for them to respect others.

It's hard to leave your child.
It's hard to take care of others besides your
child.
It's hard to see them grow without you on their
side.
It's hard to feel how much you miss them so.

Mother's selfless love.
No matter how far I am right now.
No matter what happens,

I will teach them to love and care for each
other,
in the coming days and forever.

Mother's selfless love.
To give importance to her children.
I choose to sacrifice my desire
for the needs of my children
without any thought of my well-being.

A MOTHER

As a mother,
I have loved you right from the start,
I give you comfort and peace
like a beautiful dove.
I have fulfilled every woman's desire.
Carrying an angel's life,
to be an extraordinary woman.
To be called a mother.

It brings me pride and joy,
your achievement touches me
and thrills me like no one else's can.
You give my eyes tears
and make my heart breaks at times,
but it doesn't make me feel less.
As a mother, it's not always easy.
I know I've said words,
I've done things that hurt,
frightened and confused you.

No one's ever made me
as satisfied as you being happy.
No one's made me
as proud as you living up
to your love and dedication.

No one's smile has ever warmed my heart
as your smile does.
No one's laughter fills my heart with delight
as instantly as your laughter can.
No one's hug feel
as sweet as your hugs do.
No one's dreams mean
as much to me as your dreams do.

You are a part of me,
my life and everything.
And no matter
what happened in the past.
Or what the future holds.

I will always accept you.
I will always forgive you.
I will always appreciate you
I will always adore you
I will always love you.
unconditionally.

As a mother,
I have been given life's greatest gifts.
A gift as precious as a gem.
A gift that will forever
be loved and treasured.

My children's life -
the reason why I am still alive.

BRAVERY

Life is full of surprises, yes it's true.
You never know what you need to pursue.
You never know where you will end up.
You never know how you gonna end up.

We have responsibilities to fulfill.
Sacrifice to leave our loved ones was made.
To save their future away from danger.
Thinking that our safety doesn't matter.

A bright woman seeking a father.
Being left alone looking for an answer.
Her courage develops curiosity.
Gives her an idea to go on a journey.

The journey begins and she was ready.
Recklessness brings her to dismay.

A woman has full of confidence.
Fighting spirit to overcome any challenge.
A woman with such determination,
Will never lose for any king of destruction.

Her bravery gives her power.
To break through the barrier,

Brings her to find the answer.
Finally found her long-lost loving father.

It gives her more reason to fight.
For every struggle, she might.
Using the colour of life in learning the true
light.
It's true bravery I say, that she fights for the
day,
Not without fear, but with the purpose to
appear.

SHE IS A WOMAN

She is a woman,
    like a rose with a lot of thorns,
        thorns that signify her flaws.
She might not be perfect,
    but she's beautiful and precious
        In her own simple and unique way.

She is a woman,
    she struggles in life,
        once vulnerable and so isolated.
She might lose for a while
    and manage to find her new own-self.

She is a woman,
    stronger and braver,
        spirited and committed.
She can now stand on her own,
    with so much love,
        respect and positivity
          deep within her soul.

Open your eyes!
Look at all her thorns.
Never give up on her!
Take her!

Give her life!

Take fate to rescue her!
It might be very hard.
Give yourself another chance.
She needs a chance.
To know she's worthy.

She is a woman,
      wished to be valued,
          for who she is.
Know her more deeply,
      you will never regret it.

She is a woman.
She needs someone.
She needs you.
And you alone.

MEMORIES IN MY HEART

In the end, it was just me and my thoughts,
A painful trap, long after you were gone.
Those memories we've had in the past,
Will keep going on and on.
I never stop thinking about you,
Since you went away.

I closed my eyes to fantasize,
You're a beautiful face when you were here.
I do nurture the time we did spend together,
They stayed deep inside my heart forever.

As long as I have those happy memories we
had.
I will never forget you all the way.
Even if we don't talk anymore,
Your voice is singing into my ears.

You opened my eyes to see the reality,
You cleared my worries to feel delighted,
Now you were gone, how can I disregard it?
You were the most wonderful man I've ever
met.

SIXTEEN YEARS TOGETHER

What happened to us?
I really don't understand.
We were both in love
Married and have 2 children.

What happened to us?
Where did the love go?
Will it go away?
Or is it still there?

I don't hate you!
Because I always loved you.
We don't talk,
Because there is nothing to say.

You apologized
But never keep a word.
I need to clear my mind.
I am hurting,
Because I trusted you that much.

Look at me in the eyes,
Listen as my heart cries out of pain.
Thought you were different,
But you're all the same.

What do I do?
When I am still in love with you.
Should I let you go?
To free ourselves for good?

I'll always miss you
And you'll always have my heart.
I wish I could turn back the time
When we were walking on the aisle.

"Sixteen years Together"
Promises are all made to be broken.
I wish I could change everything
For us to be better.

"MAKE YOURSELF PROUD"

When I learned I have you on my womb,
Happiness is all that I felt.
Carrying you at my very young age,
You are not planned but have never been a
mistake.

You come out to the World not hearing you
cry,
Melts my heart scared of losing you so fast.
You are truly a precious gift from above,
Thank God for trusting you to me.

Watching you grow up is like a diamond that
shines.
You've been specially made for me to love and
hold.
You are the sweetest and a very innocent child,
Your smile takes away all the pain.

Leaving you so little at 5 years old,
My heart broke into pieces,
Sacrificing for a better future.
I am so proud of how you've become.
You've grown so fast and strong.

I miss you so dearly! I love you so bad!
Longing for your hugs and kisses.
I know you're happy or having a bad day.
I wish to offer a shoulder to lean,
When feeling down and uncomfortable.

I can be your friend,
Listens to everything from your heart.
I can be your enemy if you feel so down.
I want you to keep in mind,
I am always your Mother.

I may not be a perfect Mother,
Being far away as you grow up.
Harsh and unfair sometimes,
Someday you'll realize,
I taught you well because
I do love and care.

I wish you to be a good daughter of mine.
But most of all, like a good child of God.
Work hard for your dreams to come true.
Be sweet and humble as you always do.

I may not be always at your side,
I believed you are good enough.
Can manage to stand on your own.

"Make yourself proud!"

Step up and keep going,
Wish our dreams will all come true.
Have faith, trust yourself, you'll be there,
The good Lord will do the rest.

"BE A MAN"

I love your sister before loving you!
You were not my firstborn child, which is so
true.
But the last child I have is you.
I love you and I always do!

Watching you and your sister,
Growing together was a great accomplishment.
Loving you both,
Is my biggest achievement.

Son, forgive me for leaving you so early at 4
years of age.
I hope someday you'll understand.
Your sweet smiles always heal my pain.
Warmth my heart and soul completes my day.

I wish you courage and strength
To face life challenges.
I will be there if you fall,
Hold your hand and help you stand tall.

You've been a blessing to us, it's real.
I can't promise to be here,
For the rest of your life.

But, I will protect you to the best I can.

I am so proud of how you've grown.
I may not carry you now in my arms,
I will always carry you in my heart.
I will proudly shout to the whole world,
You are my one and only son.

You are one of a kind!
You loved me as much as I do.
I can see and feel the respect in your heart.
I want you to shine bright like the sun.

There might things that help you strive.
Be my son as gentle and sweet as you are.
Never change for anyone.
Be brave and strong,
"Be a Man" of your own that you'll always be.

WE ARE FAMILY

The family bonded
          by the greatest
power of love.

No matter what,
          the family
has each other's back
          when force comes
to nudge.

Everyone appreciates,
          never command,
all for one
          and one for all.

It will never leave you
          alone suffering.

The family in itself
          love is everyone's love.
One feels sorrow,
          everyone can feel sorrow.

Any kind of struggles,
          hand in hand

38

fight together.

A promise
        to never leave
anyone alone.

If love could be
        fantasized about,
the family would be
        the strategy.

The power of family
        is a reflection of
God's forgiveness
        and splendor.

The family never
        turning our back,
and never spotting
        shamelessly.

Lending, helping hand
        and not a finger-pointing
the responsibility.

No matter what,
        a family bond can

never be broken.

Forever to eternity,
        we are family.

SIMPLICITY

I am a simple woman,
    that doesn't understand,
What's going on?
I am not glamorous or beautiful,
I am just simply me!

I have imperfections,
And that is my weakness!
When I took a good look in the mirror,
I can see a different personality!

I am a simple woman,
I don't expect to be high!
But I do know what I deserve!

I deserve to be loved!
I deserve to be respected!
I deserve to aim high!
I deserve to succeed!

I am a simple woman,
    who always get emotional!
I don't go pleasing anyone,
It's your own decision to like me or not!

41

I am a simple woman,
    who feels a heartache most of the time!
Easily melt, when family matters were all
about!

I am a simple woman,
    blessed to have some positive friends
around!
Willing to correct every mistake,
    I just made one today!

I am a simple woman!
Simplicity! Yes, it's true!
I have a lot of imperfections!
I won't change it to be perfections!
Because I would become a different person!
And not that simple woman that I am
anymore!

ENDLESS SCENERY

Looking up in the sky,
Lonely and dreaming of
endless scenery I am viewing,
Miles away from my children.

I wish to see you both through,
That beautiful scenery in the sky.
One day I will see both of you again,
Spend days with so much fun, forever.

Imaginations are all that I have,
How will I gonna make it in life?
We're both in a different part of the world,
To provide a better life for the future.

This beautiful scenery helps me feel better.
Staring above when feeling so dreary.
Someday when the dilemma is over,
Top priority is to be with you both in my arms.

THE OTHER SIDE OF ME

She is a Mother of two,
Businesswoman and wealthy.
She's able to give her
Family needs without hesitation.

She's a happy and contented wife
Of a loving and faithful husband.
She doesn't need to worry
Even if they are miles away from each other.

She has a good,
A loyal,
And a trusted friend
That doesn't make her life miserable.

She is strong,
She is brave,
Full of self-confidence,
Full of positivity in life.

I wish to accomplished
All that good quality
Of the other side of me.

PERFECT DAY

All my life, I am wishing to have a perfect day
ever.
Being with family without any kind of
destruction
Having a picnic in a very calm and quiet place
I always dream to do it on a beach specifically
on Boracay Island.

It's been so good to feel the freedom of any
stress feelings,
Focusing on my family's great memories after a
long journey to success.
Trying to relax after the long years of hard
work being away with them.
And experienced their presence and feel their
love and care.

Laughing, giggling, chatting, eating while
cooking all-day.
Coping up with all the days being far away
from each other.
Forgetting every struggle and
misunderstanding in life.
Creating good and memorable memories to
keep while I am alive.

My family is the best gift from the Heavens
above.
I will treasure it for the rest of my life, I will
truly do!
I am willing to sacrifice to give them a good
and easy life.
Without any complain, even if I always got
tired.

I wish to experience this after dealing with all
my difficulties,
Being able to pay all my debts in any kinds and
my housing loan,
When my 2 children completed their studies
with flying colors,
After I saved a sufficient amount for our family
emergency fund.

God knows what's inside my heart, I truly
believed so!
I wish I could make it until the end, I am
willing to wait!
Believing to Him to grant His full guidance,
hoping soon!
His true perfect time for me to have my very
Perfect Day!

With my loving family, that's all I am praying
for!

YOU GAVE ME LIFE

For me, you are a strong man compare to
anyone,
You sacrifice everything for the one you love.
You sacrifice your future for my Mother's
ambition.
You gave me life and I thank you for that.

I may not tell you how much I love you more
often,
I don't support your decisions most of the time
either.
Yet you gave me all the support when I needed
you most.
Thank you, *Papang*, I love you and I always do.

I am not a perfect daughter, you know that!
Being stubborn and rebellious most of the time.
You accept all my imperfections, all the time!
You love me the way I am, I am sure of that!

Once I asked for advice on the problem I had,
Should I let it go? Should I keep it?
I am tired *Papang*, please help me!
I can't handle it anymore!
I wish you can hug me the way you used to do.

You talk to me sincerely without any
hesitation.
I am your daughter but you don't even
approve of my decision,
I feel very desperate and even disliking you at
first,
Without knowing the ideas you want me to
understand.

You gave the best guidance that anyone can't,
You always think about what is best for me
and my children.
At the end of the day, you'll always make sure,
That I will follow the favorable direction for
my family.

I wish and I pray, God will give you a long life
to live.
I want to give you more love than I seldom
give.
I want you to experience how to be served by
me.
I want to feel your very warm hug that I
always longing for.

Thank you for always catching me up from my falling,
Thank you for all the support, you never fail me!
Thank you for all the care and unconditional love!
Thank you for giving me my life, I will forever be grateful!

I love you so dearly my Father dear!

FATHER'S EYES

He was my strength
when I knew I'd fall,
Always my anchor
so powerful and firm.

His face changes
when it comes to me.
His soft side,
so careless and free.

He can't give what I want,
it breaks his heart.
He knows I am stubborn,
and gets all that I want.

He supports me with everything.
He believes I'm ready
to do this on my own,

Every time I cry,
he calmed and holds me tight,
He tries to be strong,
not a tear in sight.

I'm ready to go and
have my own destiny.
To build my own family.
I'm ready to scrutinize.

He's ready to watch
his little girl's future.
It's time to let go,
sure of a journey to seize.

But now I know,
even towers can break.
When my family is almost broken,
trying to stifle my cries,
All I could see were
tears in my father's eyes.

FIRST FAILURE

An only child, alone and lonely,
Raised by loving and caring grandparents,
Grew up with cousins around,
A heart longing for a parent's love.

As a child, incredibly active, love to explore,
Started in school at a young age,
Studied generously, discovered new things,
Accomplishing academic awards was a
priority.

As a student well-focused and disciplined,
Being on a Dean's list as everyone's ambition.
Competitive, devoted to all school activities.
Motivated to attain the objectives in life.

One day, all the dreams began to vanish.
Financial difficulties were the main reason.
Three more semesters and I will succeed,
Huge failure in life existed.

Everything happens for a reason, I believe so!
I might fail my dreams of finishing my studies.
Once I have told, we should struggle the
failure,

Believe of it as a stepping stone,
That will lead you to the ultimate destination.

"HOW TO BE LOVED BY A MOTHER?"

I was just 2 years and 5days old
God took you away.
A baby's heart and mind
Melt and broke into pieces.

It's very sad to say,
I can't remember any memories.
Growing up can't fight a feeling
Longing for your love and attention.

Tears fall freely from my eyes
Like a river filled with grief.
Wishing a warm hug
From a mother's loving arms.

"*Mamang*, help, and guide me."
Those are the words I always asked.
There's an ache within my heart
That will never go away.

I wish someday I can be with you.
I can feel you so dearly.
How to be loved by a loving Mother.
I need you and I love you truly.

I WILL CHERISH YOU

Feeling so delighted,
    for the good news I had.
Can't define the feelings,
    never been imagined even once.
Now that is fulfilled,
    everything will be changed.
Change every plan,
    from now on and then.

I will be forever joyous,
    to the person who gave me trust.
Trust that I will cherish,
    until the last breath I possess.
Someone will rarely trust all the way,
    especially when you don't know each other
        in person anyway.
Seeing you on social media is just enough,
    to give you that one of a kind trust
        is more than enough.

You know how much I respect you,
    from the bottom of the heart though.
I wish to have your eagerness,
    to continue my pilgrimage to fondness.
You gave me truly much attention,

I am caressed for it without any question.
Thank you will never be enough,
   you humbly say it's nothing that's, enough!

I will forever cherish you!
The whole day is perfect!
I will honor it always!
You are the reason for everything!

SISTER FROM THE MOON

You are not my sister, yes it's true!
We are not even close, quite so true!
I know you since childhood, we both know!
We live in the same village, everyone may
know!

You knock on my door, I let you in.
You offered me the opportunity, I let myself in.
You encourage me to change my belief,
You enlighten my knowledge I feel relief.

I asked myself, why only now?
Why you didn't come earlier than I thought?
What took you so long to knock on my door?

A glanced at this photo, I saw your face in
there.
As a reminder, the darkest side will change,
In your presence, a wonderful future will
shine.
A shine I wish that will never fade.

Thank you for cheering me up, we both can do
it!

Thank you for your encouragement, yes I can
do it!
Thank you for your understanding, no one can!
Thank you for believing in me, yes I can!

You are my moon, who shines my way,
A way that almost leads me in the wrong way.
You lighten up my spirit, to go and find
myself.
And motivates me to be the best version of
myself.

AMAZING WOMAN

You're an amazing woman,
Everyone adores.
You stand firm,
With your own decision.

Your daughter is lucky,
To keep her with you.
Being an early mother,
Big sacrifice can do.

Every hardship paid off,
Seeing your daughter,
With her success,
A mother's great happiness.

Congratulations for being so strong,
Every woman would have envy for,
Having full of confidence,
And powerful determination.

REAL FRIENDS

I have my friends all the way.
Some of them may or never stay.
Few are those who knew me just then.
Come and go now and then.

I appreciate a very unique light,
Some that radiate so very bright.
They do have a personality that I love,
A blessing from heaven's above.

The thought that we get torn apart,
The thing that just breaks my heart.
You should know and feel deep inside,
Whatever happens, I'm always at your side.

Please do always know and be aware,
You are all special, and I do care.
Real friends like all of you, on this day,
Make me appreciate in a special way.

Deep within you may find,
Emotions unsaid in your mind.
Hold on tight, and don't let go.
Remember the faith, let it grow.

Of all the people throughout my day,
I wish the best for you, I say.
You, all my friends, whom I really know.
That I've met two-three decades ago.

I LOST MY FRIEND

I kept asking myself,
Where is my friend?
Is she really gone?

I miss you truly,
I wish to talk to you
Like we always do.

We had so much fun,
Laughing all the time.
Sharing secrets and problems,
Asking me to calm down.

You were like a sister,
Always offer a hand.
You are a great person,
I have so much respect for you.

When I feel so down,
I come to you for advice.
You always speak so nice,
Make me feel everything will be alright.

A friend like you
Will never be forgotten.

I wish I could see you
And feel you care again.

I wish we will always be friends!
I will always be waiting.
Hope you could remember
Our memories together.

I lost my friend
A very caring one.
I wish she will find a way
Come back and talk to me one more time.

EQUALITY

You and I will never be the same.
You grew up prosperous,
I lived an ordinary life.
Your beliefs are contrary,
to what I am fighting for.

You're much happier,
I feel like I am being left behind.
You are unique in your beauty,
Compared to my simple nature.

Everyone will never be the same.
Black, White, Asian, race, or any color.
We are not even brothers or sisters,
Not by blood nor by skin,
But by the spirit that is within,

No matter what or who we are,
Hand in hand we will live as one.
Our dear Father created us all in one.
Live in an extraordinary and everlasting life.

Let's all live happily and peacefully.
Leave the bitterness and love one another.
We are all equal, no matter what happens.

Unique equality will bind us all together.

PERFECT BEAUTY

A flower that seen very rare,
Beautiful in the eyes,
That attracts everyone,
Despite dirty roots from within.

Like most people around,
We might have the dirtiest identity to be kept
hidden,
But when we choose to survive better,
We will bloom to be the finest,
And extraordinary than anyone.

Let's be like the lotus flowers,
From the dark angle of ourselves deep within,
Let the courage be shone so brightly,
Motivate the journey and be as extraordinary
as it brings.

Show enthusiasm, boost confidence,
Enlighten the courage to its radiant strength,
Purify the personality to its perfect beauty,
That captivates positivity to arise from the
heart.

PEACE

Believe in what God has given you,
The things have lain on your heart,
Unlock what has placed within,
The potential you have inside.

Enhance your wings and fly,
Be ignited and empowered.
Don't hold back or limit yourself,
Let His power emerge within.

Take His message to guide your way,
Conquering those doubts that pull you down.
And believe who you are in Christ,
For you shall surely be transformed.

Trust yourself with all might,
God will direct you to the right path.
Let go of the past and start a new life.
For you have peace in your whole life.

The sun will shine after the heavy rains,
Preparing for a new and glorious day.
Cleanse your heart with positive minds,
Allow peace to come to guide you all the way.

A DAY IN A BEACH

Once I have told,
Going to the beach
Surely you'll find the feeling
So peaceful and comfortable.

Walking in the seaside,
Smells the wind with the breeze,
Picking up seashells
Happiness all-day out.

Feels the waves inside the water.
Sounds like the music of nature calm my heart.
Take away the sadness
Feelings from the heart.

Heavy rain pours from heaven above,
Seems like a sign to take away
Sadness, tears from the eyes
From hidden feelings inside.

Watching some children,
Playing and running around.
Friends are chatting
And playing sand games everywhere.

Sometimes you can see,
Lovers walking holding hands
Enjoying every moment
They were together.

A day at the beach is not complete,
Without catching the smooth waves.
Playing on the sand
Like you were always young.

Someday I will come back
And feel the calmness you bring to my heart.
I will always treasure
The moment I felt all day round.

DREAMING

After long hours of a tiring working day,
We take some rest and try to get some sleep.
Dreaming as we sleep,
Sounds normal to everyone.

I come to realize,
I dream of you so many times.
Two lovely little white rabbits,
Happily playing all around.

Not only once or twice,
I wonder why you'll always come back.
I wish you will bring very good luck to my life,
Better things with positive outcomes.

It reminds me to find a way
To know the meaning
For you always in my dreams.

I hope it will come true,
Positive results they said about you.
Bringing faith, and a relationship
With my love that nothing could change.

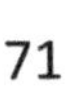

I choose to keep on going,
To the life that shows the right path.
Your presence, hopes, every happiness will
bring.
Thank you for my very calm "dream".

I LOVE MYSELF

Who am I?
I need to figure this one out.
It's frustrating not knowing me,
For myself, I'm a little bit shy.

Sitting in the corner,
Thinking for the future to come.
Failures everywhere,
So scared to be alone.

One day, I began to love myself.
Hold onto my hopes and dreams.
My fears are less than it seems.

Rain may pour heavily
The sun will shine again.
It always remains
And all the darkness will fade away.

Once I found HOPE
Encouragement was overwhelming
Began to trust me again
And do the things I loved the most.

I hold my head up high

And feel the warmth
That will remind me of
What am I truly worth?

"I love myself!"
I began to rise up
Follow all my dreams
And transform my life.

UNIQUE UNICORN

Never let anyone
tells you whom to be.

Never let anyone
make you think
you are not good enough.

You were made to be you.
Only you who truly matters.

Hold your head up
and continue to be yourself.

You are perfect,
don't give up.

Live every day
with no regrets.

Grow each day
into the person
that you were meant to be.

Be unique
and authentic

as a Unicorn
in the fields of Horses.

THINKING OF THE PAST

I want to change ME, my LIFE, my FUTURE,
but I don't know where do I begin.
If only I can turn back the time,
ten years from now.

Should I go back from my past,
to start all over,
choose the friends whom I can hang on,
to be trusted with?

A friend offers
a shoulder to lean on,
a hand to hold,
a heart to care.

Did I use my mind to think wisely,
Realized what might happen?

I truly had a soft heart, easy to melt.
I may not cope up with what happened.
Stuck with a situation that I don't know how to
get out.

I failed myself.
I fell to the ground.

It's hard to stand up.
Wake up and do it!

What life would I have if I am not here right
now?

I learned my lesson.
Dealing with mistakes.
Asking so many things.
Wipe away the regrets.

I wish I can answer all my whys.
And have the courage to start anew.
I should use my mind very gently and wisely.
To change everything into a better one.

LIGHT UP MY WAY

Be the moon that lights my way!
Be the moon that lights her way!
Be the moon that lights their way!

I am in my dark time!
I need the light that shines!

Light! Light! Light!
I need light!
To shine on my way!
To direct me to the right path!

I wish to have my moon all the time!
Willing to shine down to every one!
To shine down on me, on them, on everyone!
All over the world, no matter how far,
        and no matter where we are!

It never fails to shine down in every darkness!
It always reminds us that there's still hope,
        there's still someone out there!
A good Samaritan who's willing to be a moon
        to each and everyone who's not expecting
                anything in return.

GREAT PRETENDER

Wearing a mask!
Hiding behind!
Fool the world!
But never can fool your own!

Who are you anyway?
Do you really know?

Do not hide!
Do not pretend!
Of someone, you are not!
Show the real you!

Show your love!
You will be loved.
Show your respect!
You will be respected!

Do not say a word!
Do not rule anyone!
Show you care!
You will never be forgotten!

Unleashed your mask!
It is never too late!

Show the world you're capable!
To earn what you aiming for!

DARKNESS AT NIGHT

There was a time, I am feeling down,
Everything was darkness, feeling so alone.
Pouring heavy rain, can't make it home.
Felt everyone has left, I just want to hide.

Family was in suffering, friends can't be found,
I just want to scream, I can't find the sound.
I know it's all my fault, and I am done,
Face the reality and let the suffering be gone.

A big storm always passes, never lasts forever.
Rain will always stop; just give it more time,
Provides a way to positive weather.
Radiant and warm days still appear.

Some people may still need me
Some people may still love me.
They can warm up the soul in me,
Like the sun that shines directly on me.

I'll never be alone, no matter what was done.
God is guiding me directly to my home.
Dark clouds always pass, I believe that!
I'll always be waiting for a bright sky.

Just like the moon, give darkness at night,
New hope will shine to start a new life.
Forget all the past, forget all the darkness.
Accept a new journey, follow the right path,
That will lead and direct you to the top.

ALONE

When I was a little girl,
I was full of love and joy.
Running and playing around,
With everyone's attention.

Smile in my face,
My family would love it.
Feeling of completeness,
And everything was fine.

Time passes by,
People suddenly changed.
Once a happy face,
Turn into emotionally serious sadness.

Looking for someone,
Who truly cares.
Anyone who understands,
And offer some help.

Loneliness is truly painful,
It kills your deep emotions.
Emptiness feeling,
And grabbing you to the ground.

When I was a little girl,
I was full of love and joy.
Now my life's full of sadness,
Emptiness, and pain.

When I was a little girl,
I was never on my own.
But now I wish and pray,
I don't want to be "alone."

FEAR

I try to remember exactly what it is that I fear.
Is it the death of time or the love that I need?
Is it the carelessness that I've made
Or the truth that I can't seize the past back?

What is it that I'm scared of?
Why am I so frightened?
Is it the people I've hurt,
Or the people that will harm me?

Am I horrified by everything that I can't seem
to see?
Is it the love and trust of a friend,
Or the loss of my own family?
Is it the possibility that my life,
Can end in a tragedy?

What is it that I fear most?
What do my visions say I'm afraid of?
Is it the sun that sets but won't seem to rise?
Is it the hope that I have,
And always seems to disappear?

Is it me? Is it myself?
Can it possibly be that the thing,

I fear most is the thing that can't exist?
The things that I try to appreciate?

Is it me?
Is it myself that I try to be with when I'm
feeling bitter?
The person I'm anticipated to be?
Is that what I worry about?
I believe the thing I fear the most...
............................is me, my self.

EMPTINESS

I find myself in an empty room,
Being locked and nowhere else to go.
When I looked around, and all I can see,
Is an incredible and empty space.

I realized, did anyone notice I am here?
Did anyone concern to think about me?
It's very hard dealing with the hurt,
I feel like no one's there during all my sorrow.

I have nothing left to lose, and nothing left to
gain,
I fight through those days, with no one at my
side.
All my days are terrible, dark, stormy, cold and
grey,
Emptiness keeps growing so quickly as I
slowly fade away.

If I broke down and lost all my control,
Would you come and save me from this empty
room?
I have no courage left to go out in this sphere,
No helping hand to pull me to free myself out.

I am sad,
I am lonely,
I am irrational,
I am complicated.

For a while, I try so hard to fight away my
doubts,
So far away, I assumed they are already gone.
But I think nothing lasts forever,

The pains, darkness, tears, always find their
way,
To come and bring me to the empty side of
myself,
That I am trying to fight to get over and free
myself out.

MY OWN ANXIETY

Frighten, scared, troubled,
Sadness, depression.
Some of the words I could use
To describe my anxiety,
When they ask me what I am afraid of,
Honestly, I lie.

I would never confide the reality about you,
My true punisher and my torturer.
The scary voice inside my head telling me
badly,
Things I can't talk about for fear I'll forget who
I am.

You always tell me we are the same,
But I am not you.
You teach me to take revenge,
And let her suffer more than me.
You told me I am nothing,
I am worthless,
I am not worthy to be loved.
You pulled me down
To the lowest level of my self-depression.
You take away my self-confidence.
You teach me not to trust anyone around me.

I don't know why I listen to you?
When you force me to cry loud every time,
And throw away everything I hold.
When you said I will never listen
And trust my husband anymore.
When you tell me my family is worthless
And is going to be broken for the rest of my
life.

I should not listen!
I should ignore you from the very start!
You never helped me anyway!
You make everything worst!
Even worst than ever!

I have had enough difficulty.
I am not vulnerable!
I never was.
I never will be.
You are me!
You are only my thoughts,
You can never defeat me!

I am stronger than you!
I am a survivor!
I learned my lesson!

And I will survive.
And I will love myself.
And I will not let go.

EMBRACE OUR NATURE

See the sunrise
    from the east,
 Like a diamond
    shines very brightly.
The new hope
    for the new morning
      it's fascinating.

The freshest air
    from the universe,
Leaves from trees
    dance to its rhythm.
Conveys calmness
    and the feeling is even lighter.

Feel every drop of rain
    from heavens above,
Gradually it touches
    the soft skin.
Feel the cold water
    that soothes your feelings.

Watch the sunset to the west,
Another meaningful day has passed.
Calm and soothe your mind,

for tomorrow another day
    to face a new challenge in life.

Embrace our nature,
That gives us pleasure.
Everything will be productive,
For an extraordinary future.

CHANGE FOR HUMANITY

Change is never easy,
Changing oneself is very hard,
In these hard times, we need to change.
Change our belief,
Change our perspective,
Change our personality,
For the good of humanity,
Not only in one place,
It includes all over the world.

We are all suffering our tough times,
Embracing the world's scariest virus
everywhere.
No one can detect where it all comes from.
We need to change our selves,
For us to be safe at all times.

People are dying,
People crying out,
From all the suffering.
Illness, hunger, deadly disease,
Eating away at humanity,
From the inside out.

Corruption and violence

As never seen before.
Noncompliance of authority,
The immorality of every kind.
All of these things are happening,
We need to understand too,
We must do our part,
To make our lives competitive.
Don't give in to humanity's voracious distress.
Start to make the right determination for
yourselves.

INNOCENT SMILE

Amid the darkness,
    a heart was been torn into pieces,
a mind was blown somewhere.

Nights full of fears,
    emotions full of dismay,
future was uncertain.

Attitude with anxiety,
    a feeling cannot understand,
self-discipline was very inadequate.

An innocent smile
    from a very sweet little boy
changed everything.

Whatever emotions you feel,
    sad, happy, scared, or lonely.

Seeing him smile at me,
    I will forget all the burdens
deep inside of me.

Whatever the circumstances may give you,
    difficulties and burdens in your life,

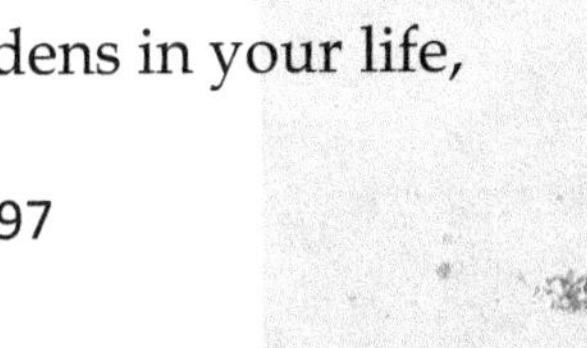

find a way to smile.

It will lessen your desperate emotions inside.
It will lead you to a brighter side of yourself.

Smile to yourself,
     smile to everyone.

It is on how you give a smile to someone,
     it will truly find a way to coming back to
you
when you badly need it.

Those simple innocent smiles
     that means nothing to someone,
give you the courage to start a new life.

New hope to begin and keep going.

THE GOODBYE

I have been there before you were born,
Preparing for the things you'll be needing.
You are not mine, yes it's true.
You are not from my womb,
I didn't deliver to you either.

In my heart, you are a daughter of mine,
A precious gem that I will take good care of.
You've grown up incredibly fast,
Beautiful and sweet little angel you've become.

You loved me sending you to playschool,
Learning kids songs we used to sing.
Sleepless and stressful nights paid off,
Watching you every day for six years of my
life.

Suddenly, your mother's attitude changed,
Being you neared me she has never been
approved.
Screaming of things not really understandable,
Changing her personality never stops.

The home has never been good as before,
Decided to resign earns my depression.

I don't want to leave you,
I will definitely miss you.

Seeing those tears from your eyes,
Hugging so tight, you never stop.
Whispering Goodbye to you,
Is really a difficult thing to do.

I step out and closed the door,
Crying out so loud, never care for neighbors to hear.
It's hard to go, leaving you my not-born-child.
I dream of us meeting again.

WALK AWAY

Rejoice, the whole world rejoices with you
Cry, and you cry all alone.
Sadness in a place that can borrow happiness.
But the efforts are enough of their own.

Scream loud, but no one else can hear.
Murmur, it's dancing in the air.
Loud echoes bring joyful sound.
Smashing from prolonged care.

Rejoice, and everyone will seek you.
Dismay, grief, everyone left and gone.
Be content, for who stayed.
Be sorry, for all who left.
Alone, accept life challenges.

Rejoice, the whole world goes by.
Walk, slowly, take some baby steps.
Succeed and give, be free, willingly.
No one else will go to help you!

Help yourself!
Free yourself!
Walk away!
Build a new life!

New destiny!
New beginning!
Be simple, with humility!

WILD AND FREE

She walks, hops, and runs
through the green grass.
Young, wild and free.
Her innocent and sweet smile,
made my heart rejoices with glee.

Her heart was pure and loving,
Her eyes as fierce as a crow,
Her voice as sweet as the humming,
of the birds down in the hallway.
Everything she knew was happy,

As she grows,
just like the pretty butterflies,
Freely flies to explore
the beauty of the world.
Experience every ups and down,
Discovering new things to be wild.

Fly high sweet child of mine,
In your arms open wide
Embrace the fresh air.
Witness the changes.
Freeing your inner beauty
to be open wild.

IN YOUR EYES

I hate what you did to me!
I hate how you hurt my back!
I hate that it took all these years
to get back a broken me.

Do you know, what you did to me,
not only physically but mentally!
Do you know how,
this set me back spiritually!

In your eyes, you are perfect!
In your eyes, you are divine!
In your eyes, you are a goddess!
In your eyes, you are innocent!

It is all a lie,
I can see your fraud.
You're too much,
I can feel every bitterness
It is hard to deal with it

Give it a break.
Take a deep breath.
Release the anger!
Release the hatred!

With all your imperfections,
I have loved you, we all do!
Accept it, and start to mend the broken soul.
Forgive yourself and be fair.
Eyes will never lie.
It speaks faithfully.

BEAUTY IN LIFE

How could anyone dare?
To catch and to hold you
Against your sobriety will?

They should admire you
and let you have your fill.
Of flying here and flying there,
gathering up your daily strength
of nectars from the flowers bright,
from early morning until night.

You are so beautiful,
with so many colors rare,
it hurts my heart
when one dies,
Yet, does anyone truly care?

For you represent new birth,
from chrysalis until you die,
you beautify the earth.
Thank you, pretty one.
You made my childhood memories
so special and bright.

Fly high and shine so bright.

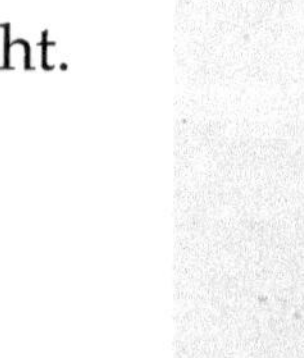

Give meaning to every color,
That gives all the beauty in life.
Make sure you do it no harm.

IF ONLY

If only you will see,
What my eyes see,
That you need to see,
And not letting others see,
Those things pass to you blindly.

If only you just hear,
What my ears hear,
That you need to hear,
And ignoring what others hear,
Some people do not even think to bear it.

How can you even say,
That everything you say,
Were those things all true like you always say,
Everyone's wrong like what they say,
So many things never come their way.

I want you to know, of all those times,
I silently cried, scream at night sometimes,
I want you to know, of all those hurt times,
It painfully resides in my heart most of the
time.

Would it reach your ears even before?

Would you at least listen some more?
Would you care for me even more?
Would you still treat me just like before?
Like I'm not even there to exist forevermore?

I wanted you to see, everything you've missed.
Scars on my arms and legs, but by you get
dismissed.

I wanted to show you, how you slowly break
my heart.
Would you notice it, or pretend to care for my
heart.
I wish you understand, what's going on on my
part,
Right in front of your eyes, my life is falling
apart.

Maybe it's time for you to at least realize,
I have been alone, in this place without you
even realize.
Hoping for you to come, and release me from
the dark paradise.
Our true love will live happily and forever in
that beautiful paradise.

WHY?

I am here without no one realize it.
Why can't people see the real me?
Am I not as beautiful as others?

I tried so hard to be perfect as I can be.
I knew for sure that I'm fresh, young, quiet,
and shy.
But I'm just an ordinary living thing which
many pass by.

Why?
I am being alone and left behind.
Why can't people just take the time?
Sit with me, I'll listen to every word you tell.

Tell me your favourite thing to do and I'll
always listen.
Tell me your burdens and ill comfort you with
my fragrance.
They see me as mysterious, sweet, funny, and
smart.

You may not expect me to cheer you up the
very first day.

It takes time, but trust me, I'll soon have a lot to show up.

Why?
I am being ignored most of the time.
Why can't people wait and get to know the real me?
I'll assure you I'd be more unique than you first did see.

SOAR HIGH MY BUTTERFLY

As I continue watching you grow
from that small and simple
who knows nothing at all.

You simply search and explore
how you continue your journey
independently.

I never want to intrude
and interrupt.
I let you find your path
to finally find your destiny.

I love seeing you flying,
with your small,
colourful and so glamorous wings.

When you fall,
you never hesitate to go back
and spread your wings some more.

You never give up
on every struggle you encountered.

I will continue to be there,

support and guide you all the time.

I wish you to continue
and improve flying high.

Soar high my butterfly.

Spread your wings
and don't be afraid to fall back down.

Keep spreading your wings
with your love and eagerness.

Soon you will be there!

In that place,
you are aiming so hard.

I will forever be proud!

As a friend,
a sister,
a counselor,
and a mother
who will love you
unconditionally.

I SEE THE MOON

Inspired by Sarah Kay
https://youtu.be/7Iv2nZnZOrM

"I see the moon and the moon sees me,
The moon sees somebody that I don't see
God bless the moon and God bless me:
And God bless that somebody that I don't see."

Beautifully painted in the sky,
For everyone to see the light,
From the moon shines so bright,
It always glows in our dark path.

Always been there when we need it.
Keep following me wherever I go.
To the East,
To the West,
To the North,
To the South.
Reminding me to never give up.
Just keep on going until I reach
The destination I am dreaming of.

I wish you to guide me as I go through my
journey,

Through your light, I am being enlightened.
Through your light, I find my way out.

May you give light to all whom I love most,
May you shine on someone's dark life,
May you continue to lead their way to
goodness,
May you be their lamp in searching what they
are aiming for,
May you be their healing power when they feel
weak.

Under your glowing brightness,
I will walk through it as I search for myself.
For sometimes, I am being lost,
Going back to the things I've been hurt the
most.

As long as I see the moon,
In the darkness of my night.
I will never lose my hope,
I will find my way to rise again.

HE

He is the man I loved.
He is the man you loved.
He is a man in our dreams,
powerful and courageous.

With his manliness,
he has a soft heart
that only people close to him know.
He's willing to give everything that he has.

There are times he can't hide his emotions.
Accepting every harsh word
from peoples around.
Sacrificed every hard work for all he loved.

Overcome every challenge in life
in exchange for his happiness.
One day, he was sitting alone
and isolated into nowhere.

Nobody care to notice where he is now.
Nobody care to know how he is doing.
Nobody realizes his worth and goodness.
Nobody understands and appreciates him.

He is a man, with strong determination.
Decide to be brave and continue his mission.
To show the world how he changed and
improved.
And be the man of every woman's dreams.

SHE NEEDED YOU

She's beautiful with her moral and honour
Her soul radiated beyond compare
But she was nothing without you as his vapour
To nourish the roots of her fear it's so rare

If you were not there, she was just a simple
flower
Withering away from her true existence
She needs you to give her a shower
So her beauty could go beyond the distance

Without your presence, the climate, tides
change
She would just be cleaned and washed to the
sea.
And so she made sure you will stay within her
range
And you always holding onto her so
gracefully.

When you held her, it's so wonderful she grew
True love and unique beauty started to
transcend
It was then, both of your heart and souls knew
You would become more than just a friend.

In your absence, her life would never exist
There would be no affection and love ever
share
Until you embraced one another, and no one
could resist
To reveal how much you both truly love and
care

A LONG AND LASTING LOVE

You are the reason why I am still alive
You gave me the reason to survive

You are the reason why I want to fight more
You gave me angels to be loved and adore

You are my best enemy yet my only true love
You gave me everything that I asked from
above

You'll go on thru far beyond the horizon
sailing
You'll be back someday, I am still here waiting

You'll go on with my sincerity and our dearest
dove
You'll always be my long and lasting love

WHY ME?

Sitting on the edge
Thinking of the reasons
for everything behind
Too many questions
playing on my mind
Why you're still holding on
to the memories
that I kept beneath
the ground

Why me?
Why not her/him?
Why not them?
What is that you found in me?

I have no wings to fly
I have no reason to jump high
I walked away silently
I moved on quietly

Oh yes!
I am here living
in a friendly niche
Surrounded by angels
with no wings attached

I have my mind
so peaceful and calm
Thinking of nothing
but love and harmony
Confidently full of energy
Loving myself
beyond my limitation

I wish you to do the same
Live your life at peace
Yes! Sit back and relax
Imagine yourself
Sitting on that edge
Acceptance
is all that matters

SAIL TO NOWHERE

Sail with me my darling
Let's go somewhere
A place that is new to us
Where we can start
A brand new life
Away from trouble
Away from hatred
Away from greediness
Away from enviousness
Away from everyone
I want you to live
In a peaceful place
Where you can grow
With elegant grace
Full of love and respect
Full of happiness and wisdom
To face the world with courage
And build your memories
That will last forever
And you will be very proud

THE KINGDOM

At this moment,
I am in the process of searching
for the missing piece in my life.
Looking for the right key
to unlock the door of my kingdom
and steal back all the lost time.
I am searching, looking,
restless scanning every hole and gap,
lying awake all night,
dreamless empty existence.
My poor broken heart
from years and years,
I let the laughter fall
onto my small deaf ears.

No happiness is enough.
No satisfaction can be felt.
We are all searching for something
to heal ourselves,
yet no medicine is strong enough.
The right and a perfect key
can ever be turned to give us
what we aspire the most to give us
what we yearn for and strive for.
The thing that I want is a hallucination.

My perceptions are deformed.
All are worth what I rate it.
All are categorized by how I place them.
Hunting and chasing what cannot be found,
instead of deciding on to be satisfied.
Wishing for what I do not have,
a dream that cannot be
a masterpiece of mirages
all too soon I would believe.

When will I begin and start to accept
what is here in my life?
Right here!
Right now!
The present-day in which I live.
Not the past or future ahead.
When will I stop searching
and agree that I don't need more?
Not anymore!
When will be the time
I learned to satisfy with what I have.

Only then I will find
what I've been looking for.
The good I have is here,
yet I keep looking on,

never realizing what I had,
until it is all gone.
And now,
I am in a place,
where I cannot find myself anymore.
I cannot see the kingdom in my dreams.
The kingdom
I am searching for all my life.

I am nowhere!
Nowhere that nobody
could be found.

SWEET BUTTERFLY

It's been a while
I haven't seen you around
Flapping your wings
Flying all around
I've watched you
When I'm feeling blue
I'd talk to you
When I'm sad and in pain
You bowed your head
And humbly mend
Your broken heart
You're one of a kind
Now, you are here
Beautiful
So lovely
Graceful
So elegant
Wonderful
So extraordinary
You give colors to our life
Fly high my sweet butterfly
You developed yourself
So fair and fascinating
Show us what you got
Show the world your colors

It's your time to shine and fly

I AM HERE

I am here!
I want to live within the moment,
to feel all that I can to love
and cherish life for all it's worth,
for everything I am.
I wish to see what's right in front of me,
to vision crystal clear,
to face what's waiting there for me,
and never feel indecisiveness or fear.

I am here!
I wish to wake up each day
with thanks and gratitude,
and all my life may be to feel
that astonishment the world enfolds me.
I wish to welcome every stranger,
wide-open arms, heart, and mind.
I'll always stand for what is right,
all the courage I can find.

I am here!
I'll forgive myself for my mistakes
while forgiving others theirs.
I'll never grow indifferent,
I'll always strive to care.

I will never forget what matters,
the theory and idea of every day,
and live each precious moment,
a kind and loving way.

I am here!
This moment now is everything,
nothing matters but only today,
I'm willingly grasping it,
never let it slip away.
I'll treasure every second on my way.
And now, it passes all so quickly,
last one chance is all we get.
I'll always remember,
that a life of wasted moments
is a life filled with regrets.

Line Breaker Poem

SUNSET

Like the sunsets
Beautifully painted in
the sky, you love to stare,
sadness in your way
seems everything
go to ending.

It's darkness,
fading eventually;
the sun shines so brightly.
It's a reminder
whatever happened;
life can still
be glorious
in the end.

I'M A ROCK

I'm a rock!
Do you want
to break me?
Go ahead!
Scorch me.
I'm a rock!
Do you want
to damage me?
Go ahead!
Beat me.

I'm a durable rock.
Go ahead!
Abandon me.
I will shine all alone.
Will never break,
turn to ash, nor decay.
I'm a rock!
I can survive.
I am significant.
Because I'm a rock.
I'm a rock!

Imagery Poem

A RIVER WITHIN

Eyes will never lie
It's hidden the emotions deep within
When I feel joyous and weak
I felt the moisture that rolling
down on my cheek

Can taste salty and warm,
Might be big or small.
And when I am strong,
You won't come out at all.

When I am in pain
And too much to take.
When I am sad,
And my heart starts to break.

I can always feel you,
When the time I am panicked,
When the time I am so angry.
You'll show up here and there,
When enough is what I've had.

133

Sometimes when I am scared,
You were there as a sign of fear.
I always feel you when you're coming,
Whether far or near.

You may come along
When I hear my favorite song.
Sometimes you just show up
When I've been strong for too long.

I wanted to fly away.
I know inside I am a mess.
I am longing for a brighter day.
Wondering,
How can I dry the river
If I can't stop it from flowing?

I AM HERE, ALONE

Resting on my bed at night,
Alone and thinking about why I am here.
I have so much love and care to lend.
Did anyone notice my presence?

I met a guy who said he cares for me,
The care that I never felt for long ago.
He manipulated my weaknesses,
He knows how to play all along.

There is so much hurt I feel,
So much anger trapped inside.
I wish my mom were here,
with her tender care.

I have no one to talk to.
Crying seems to be the only way.
Then I realized, all a lie,
Just like the way I smile every day.

I know outside I'm smiling;
It's the face I fake for everyone,
Inside, my soul is crying,
There is nothing else I can do.

I know my family loves me.
I'm in their memories when needed.
I'm sick of feeling like I am worthless,
No one understands as I leave.

I lay in bed and asked myself once more,
What the hell I'm doing here.
Wake me up from this dream!
And let me just disappear!

A MASK, NO MORE

I wish someday will come
Even if I'm wearing a mask
And try to hide in a crowd
Everyone will recognize me
My unique personality

Everyone can;
    see my illusion
    hear my voice
    read my mind
    do my actions

Dealing with things greatly
When someone stares at me
Quite close or even from afar
They can see the real me
Without a doubt
The one and only ME

Volta Poem

COMPLICATED

The complicated thing
 I'll ever do,
Let go of you,
 not hearing your side.

And look forward
 instead of recalling my past,
I wonder how long
 this broken heart will last.

I guess everything
 you ever said was a lie,
I'm going to move forward,
 or at least I'm going to try.

I wonder how many times
 should my heart crack
 before it shatters?
Does it even matter to you?

I've sat and cried
 over you way too much,
Just wishing one more time

138

I could feel your touch.

Thinking those days
 we've been through.
Giving us one more chance
 to be fairer.

But you don't care,
 and neither should I.
Now, you were gone,
 without even saying goodbye.
So I'm going to move on,
 or at least I'm going to try.

FRIEND NO MORE

I'm a naive woman,
I met you in my dark days.
Sad being alone,
 struggling in life.

Together with a great
 and extraordinary time,
For you bring the sun
 that shines on me.

Nurtured me with knowledge
 and experience.
Boosting my self-awareness
 from people around.

Teaching me to fight
 for my right,
Always offer a hand
 when needed.

But then suddenly
 you just faded away,
In the toughest part
 of my life.

Leaving me a burden
 that I was not sure,
Dealing with it
 seriously in the future.

Yet hoping your heart
 will be touched and be healed,
We can still remove the darkness,
 and bring brightness once more.

Terra Rima Poem

A CHILD'S WISH

Lord, I want to speak with you from the heart.
It is not always easy to follow your way.
Do things right with my great brave heart.

Fighting with my chaos from yesterday.
It brings much unhappiness that can't be
denied.
I always complain it is my fault anyway.

I want to follow you, almost everything I tried.
Yes, it just seems to me, if I remember right.
I wish to obey your rules until the day I died.

Follow you that shed a lot of light.
Life could be as blessed when I do what you
conveyed.
Blessings along my journey will shine bright.

The wonderful world we could have if we all
prayed.
I need you, and I promise you to be obeyed.

MY CHILDREN'S VALUE

I am a mother with kids as strong as me.
Raised full of love as much as I can give.
Leaving them at a young age hurts me.

Sacrificed everything for us to live.
Providing their needs to avoid strife.
This hardship will soon be over, I believe.

Overcoming fears of being far and an alone
wife.
Teaching them to stand firm, to be
independent.
To reach their biggest dreams in life.

No one will help in their self-improvement.
Never try to do something that leads to
disconnect.
For their future's biggest achievement.

Ignoring misconducts that lead them to be
imperfect.
And always understand how to earn
everyone's respect.

MY GRANDMA

My heart breaks and felt so much pain.
Thinking that in my life, I always pretend.
The sky is full and drops a lot of rain.

My secret-keeper, mother, and best friend.
Always showed me right from wrong.
Never tried to give up on me, till the end.

The day of your life ends, everything went
wrong.
 It's hard for me to see you and say my
farewell.
Love and care for me that you kept for so long.

The day you died, my heart fell.
Maybe someday we will meet again in the sky.
I believed the Lord took you as your moment
went so well.

I wish, the Lord has let me say the right
goodbye.
I wish you will watch me still until the day I
die.

Simile Metaphor Poem

I AM NOT PERFECT

You may give me all those criticisms.
With your bitterness, hatred heart.
You may humiliate me like rubbish dirt.
But still, like a human, I'll rise.

Does my simplicity upset you?
Why are you so eager to hurt me back?
Is it because I choose not to speak and just
smile?
And I choose to keep moving forward to what
I love to do.

Just like the birds, the eagles,
With wings that freely fly.
Just like the fondness, the appreciation.
Being simple, I'll rise.

Did you want to see me stumbling?
Turning around with broken wings?
Head is bowing down like a bamboo tree.
And weakened by losing my self-confidence.

145

Does my happiness offend you?
Don't you take it personally!
Because I laughed so hard like I always do
To furlough all my unhappiness.

You may hurt me with your harsh words!
You may stare at me with your angry eyes!
You may slay me with your bitterness pride.
Like magic, I'll rise.

Does my positivity upset you?
Does it make you surprised?
That I am simply moving on slowly.
As if nothing just happened.

I Will go somewhere I can act freely.
Stop the quest that pioneers the pain.
I am just a human, I can feel some sorrow.
Continuously hurting, but still, I'll rise.

I am not perfect, I am authentic than anyone.
Give up what I had in the past, it makes my life
at peace.
Into that darkness that continuously fading.
And still, I'll rise.

Bringing the love and faith that my trusted
friends gave.
I am a simple woman who's dreaming,
Hoping for life so peaceful.
That will bring joy and contentment,
To trust herself and to love humanity.

BROKEN

I am in so much pain,
My heart is broken.
My life is ruined,
My soul has been damaged.

What happened to us?
We used to be so in love!
I never believed that this was real,
Never thought that I could feel.

I trusted you with my heart,
You promised to care for me.
But you just lied,
You broke it into many pieces.

I thought you are one of a kind!
That is not true!
Everything is falling apart,
It's ripping my heart.

I have so much anger that built up,
I have to get rid
Everything is happening so fast,
How long will it last?

I am sorry for everything,
But the damage has been done.
The heart is already broken,
And it's hard to put them back together again.

FEAR IN DARKNESS

Days of endless trials,
Ending up to a self depression.
It will never go away,
Seems nobody cares.

The darkness surrounds me,
It's getting so cold.
I am all alone,
No one else to hold.

My world is empty,
Everyone's left.
My heart is crying,
No one bothers to care.

Feeling I was left behind,
Not being loved by anyone.
No one cares to understand,
No one even tries to listen.

I wish I could change,
I could make it better.
I wish for another chance,
You will come and save me.
From MYSELF!

150

My fear in the darkness,
Is always in my heart.
I hide them over and over,
Pretending to be someone
I am not.

Forget all the pain in my heart
Hiding deep inside.
Someday, a time will come,
All the fears will be gone.

EXTRAORDINARY FEELING

I love to smile at everyone that can hide
A million tears keeping behind
Sometimes I feel happy and feel hurt so deeply
Pain and misery fall from the sky
I try to ignore it, but still, it gets by

Encircled by memories of what could have
been
The hatred screams under my skin
Pulsing through my veins, the anger I feel
Wounds break open as soon as they seal

Darkness surrounds me with every step I take
I manage a smile, but do you know it's fake?
I laugh so hard when people talk to me
But inside I'm dying, wishing they could see

I'm unusual inside as I am the same
Wish they could sense they're not to blame
I know the truth, but it's locked in my heart
And now more than ever, it's tearing me apart

I believe that time is a good healer
All the burdens will fade sooner or later
I can smile like a star that twinkles

Or maybe like the ocean that gently flows

I am not perfect but I am learning to be better
I am extraordinary from the others
I can be as precious as a gem to be treasured
A diamond shines that always be remembered.

Personification Poem

REFLECTION OF TRUTH

I am uniquely fragile.
Born with a silver spoon
and best etiquette.
I do not misjudge.
Whatever I see,
I comprehend it instantly.
With all my honesty,
embraced it with love and care.

I am not harsh,
I am only sincere,
Most of the time
I ponder on the opposite wall.
It is bright, with marks.
I looked at it for so long.
I believe it is part of my heart.
But it twinkles.
Expressions and darkness,
Separate us over and over.

Now I am like a little lake.
A woman bows over me.
Seeking my norms for what she is.

154

Then she turns to those untruths,
the sunlight or the moonlight.
I see her back,
reveals and reflects it faithfully.
She gives me tears
and confusion of hands.
I am significant to her.
Now and then, she comes and goes.

Each morning,
it is her face that replaces the darkness.
In me, she has drowned a young girl,
and in me a grown woman.
Rises toward herself day after day,
like a terrible fish.

Alliteration Poem

MOTHER'S WORTH

A mother, simple and bold.
Need to be as strong as no one to hold.
Worthy to give the best before being old.

A mother's held and hold, shape and mold.
Choose to carry and hold life, till getting old.
Sometimes scold you, mend, wash and fold.
Always care for all within the fold.
Mother's worth beyond a world of gold.

Forever blessed a mother's hold.
A mother provides and sacrifice unfolds.
Selflessly mothers serve tenfold.
Ignoring self desires and give their own.

No book can tell the stories told.
Of how a mother's make them whole.
Eternal wealth, a mother bestows.

Forever blessed a mother's hold.
A Mother reflects Mary's role.
A humble woman turned marigold.

A vibrant gift, a beautiful soul.

Since the mother's touch is manifold.
In various ways it lifts, upholds.
Though pierced of heart, she onward goes.
Forever blessed a mother's hold.

Blessed is the mother's courage as a whole.
As they possess an extraordinary heart and
soul.
A mother's worth will never be compared to
them all.
Selfless love from a mother is an amazing role.

BROKEN HEART

It does hurt and I am hurting deep inside.
So painful it is, and I am in deep pain.
I feel unwanted by the people I adore.
Loving someone who never loves me in return.

All my life, I feel lonely not being loved.
Never be complete and always not contented.
I am broken and I always feel broken-hearted.
I am not accepted nor appreciated.

It's like a pill to intake, that kills me inside.
It's like the deepest wound never had a chance
to cure.
It's like a thorn, that throbs into my heart.
It's like an arrow that almost harms my soul.

I do believe, time heals a broken heart.
Self-love and self-awareness lessen the
sadness.
A broken heart will surely find a way.
To ease the pain and be loved once again.

Lipogram Poem

NO! I WON'T STOP!

I find myself, sitting in the corner,
Being isolated, alone, and empty!
Feeling so senseless,
I do not know how long it gonna be.

I had done wrong,
once, twice, many times.
I admit it!
I accept it!
I needed to be more strong.

I am fine!
I am done!
I feel better!
I know for real,
it's only for a matter of time.

No one can feel the pain!
No one can see
how deep the damage it brings.

Now, I feel the emptiness.
No one cares!

159

Nobody knows!

I need to pretend,
I am strong and brave.
Overcoming the emotions I felt.
Yet deep inside I am aching.
Pain that no one can heal.

Inspiration came!
Enlightens my mind
and shines my dark path.

Only then I realized,
I need to stand firm!
I don't want to feel
being alone for one more time.
I need to keep moving forward!
Move forward with my mission.
And find where do I belong.

I am a simple woman!
I made a mistake!
I failed once more!
I need to concentrate!

I am worthy,
and that is all I know!

I have many reasons to fight
and believe
I can stand on my own!

No! I am not weak!
No! I won't confess!
No! I won't forsake!
No! I won't stop!

Without Uu

I PROMISE MYSELF

I promise myself to forget the past!
I promise myself to start a new path!
I promise myself to be more motivated!
I promise myself to be the best version of
myself!

Be simple, be extraordinary, be real.
I want to learn how to overcome, my critic.
Love myself as I never do it before.
Believe myself to be better than before.

It's time to act, and move forward,
Embrace the positive mindset of people who
care,
Concentrate on how to achieve every goal,
A good personality is where destiny depends.

I am who I am, and this is who I shall forever
be.
I will do good things for others as long as I can
be.
I do not care what others think of me.
Whether like me or not, that all depends on the
option.

Accept me for who I really am, that's what I
say.
To the people talking bad things while I am
away.
I am confident, I never do anything wrong.
Respect others if want to receive respect from
them.

I Promise Myself I will Love myself till the end.

Without Uu

163

GOOD NIGHT

Imaginations are in my mind.
So sensible and kind.
At night when I am alone.
Thinking for next the day to come.

Dreaming of good things in life
The reason why I am still alive.
All the things that amaze me.
That probably change my life.

The night is indeed so special
Looking above in the sky.
So many stars shining so bright.
Relaxing my emotions in a while.

Moon radiantly glowing in the dark.
Makes a difference for a day so hard
I close my eyes and dream for tomorrow.
I embrace the night with love glowing.

I can choose great dreams tonight.
The way I want to be, as to how it will be.
I will let the moment standstill.
Giving great meaning to end.

The night takes away all the pain.
Gives me hopes for a new start.
Sleep well and have a very good night.
Feeling so fresh and relax,
ready to welcome a new day!

Without Uu

NEVER REGRET

Dare me! And I will surely accept it!
I may be useless in their eyes,
my thinking may be insufficient
in what they are aiming at.

At least, I tried my best.
At least, I give my all.
At least, I surrender my all.
I am better than them.
Believe it! It is true!

Am I qualified with the principle being
implied?
Am I really useful as they always said
Did anything else wish my presence
Am I just being desperate
Seeing things that they never see
Hearing screams that they never hear

I am there every time I am being needed.
I was there every time I have been asked.
It gives me much pain and suffering.
Believing in lies spreading in the air.
It brings me heartache that I never presumed.

Until when they will be a victim
Until when they will use the human mind
Until when they will be wicked

I will never regret the time I made up my
mind!
I have been awakened by an Angel.
It's time, I'll rise high!
And live thy life, let all lies fly.
Explain the attitudes and give rise to the truth.
Be free! Be very free!

Without Oo

THAT GIRL

Whom you thought knows nothing.
As I can do no good.
I was just nothing.
Nobody gonna stays with.

That girl

Whom you thought knows nothing.
Stay away from you and stood up.
Wishing nothing but to stay calm.
Amidst all the chaos, I am still strong.

That girl

Whom you thought knows nothing.
Do not wish to justify anything.
Allowing you to build big walls.
Organizing your squad to punch my back.

That girl

Whom you thought knows nothing.
With all your criticisms,
you do nothing but to annoy.
I withstand, ignoring your foolish mind,

I am candid truthful in all my actions.

That girl

Whom you thought knows nothing.
You can find it so quickly.
Stays in your mind,
until you won't allow it moving on.

That girl

Whom you thought knows nothing.
I am not that girl you know now,
I am significantly transformed.
I am proud of who I am right now.

Without Ee

LIFE IS INCREDIBLE

Life is so wonderfully incredible.
Be mindful, be conscious.
It is full of mysteries, huge incredible gifts,
Life is full of surprises, yes it's true.

Don't hide, never ignore things behind.
Give yourself time to see and believe.
Open your eyes, look into the horizons,
The sun setting down until nobody sees.

Look into those impressive flowers.
For a moment, peeked on by the butterflies.
Countless colors which exist,
It will surely uplift your spirits!

However, life is now one big test,
Just for you to become the best.
Women competing with women,
Men competing with men,
Running from one to the other end,

Go out, see the sunrise up in the sky,
Witness the clouds while they freely move.
See those trees how do they thrive.
They're not in there just to survive,

There is so much more to itself.

They will rise!
There will be Life!
Incredible life!

Without Aa

SHE

Look at her!

She never believes in herself.
She was vulnerable and helpless.
She has less self-confidence.
She was empty and knows nothing.

Look at her now!

See the beauty in her pretty eyes,
See it glows that shine like the sunrise.
Her smile opens up the cloudy skies,
Her laughter delights butterflies.

Look at her once more!

She walks elegantly while all astonished eyes
stare.
She is a thorn-less rose without comparison.
She has traveled far and almost reaches her
destination.
She is a woman full of confidence and
inspiration.

Look at her in the future!

A woman, everyone recognizes her identity.
A woman that exquisitely great.
A strong, independent, fearless, bold!
A successful woman with a good heart.

Without Qq

Ode Poem

ODE TO MY FATHER

A powerful
and heroic soul
who guides
and protect me
from life's challenging
threat
The reason
for who I am
right now
who nurture me
how to be as good as
my mother was before
keep her personality exists
as I grow up

sacrifice his happiness
for me to survive,
he strives so hard
to give what I need - to live
My knight in shining armour
willing to fight
for what is right
for me and everyone
at all times
Your strength
is my courage
You are my hero
I will follow in your footsteps
to be simple,
humble and kind.
Following what my heart speaks up
and always rise
every time I stumble.

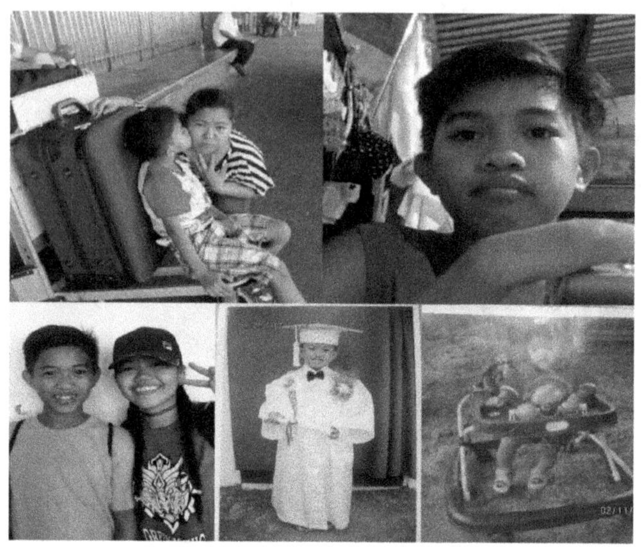

ODE TO MY YOUNG MAN

My little boy
you gave me a lot of joy
as God's given you to me
with a special role
in me and the whole family

As you grow up
you accept brighter
than the stars
glowing in the universe

You squeeze away
the sorrow and make me forget

my pain

You show me the sun
when we're walking in the rain
You are so special
in so many ways

You are my alarm clock
every time I fell into
my deep sleep
You always remind me
to get up and don't let my self
be locked in an empty room

God entrusts you to me,
I will protect and guide you
till my last breath
in this wonderful world
we are living in

ODE TO MY YOUNG LADY

You are my angel
who has no wings
You bring joy
and happiness to my life
Your smiles brighten up my days
You are a jewel
that will be treasured forever

A sweet soft
and pure innocent soul
Gives me the reason
to continue my existence
I see that lights within your spirit

trying so hard to do what's right

Those memories
I will keep in my heart
you will be forever
my sweet little girl
even you've grown up so fast
My angel who has no wings
sent from heaven above

You are my sunshine
with a sweetness that won't end
You are my best friend
and always cheers me to try my best

ODE TO MY ANXIETY

What are you doing here?
Yes! Here!
Not there! Here!
Why are you here?
You keep on following me

You keep looking
at every angle of my body
Maybe you look better
if you lose some weight
Are you saying I am ugly fat?
Damn! Did you just smile at me
or your laughing so hard?

Am I not look beautiful?
Did you just say yes?
No, I am prettier than you
Oh common
Stop comparing

Now, all her friends
are looking at me
And they are all
laughing at me now

180

I need to leave now
I need to move and go
I need to get out of here

Bye laughing lady
and her friends
Wait, did I forget something?

Forget it
I need to end this
I need to say GOODBYE

Couplet Poem

TO LIVE

How far will I'm going to live
It depends on how I believe

The integrity of life learned
Some ways others help are allowed

Sometimes we all live in joy
Thinking that we need to enjoy

What belongs to our mother earth
And all those things that were made for mirth

How does nature smiles within us
Seeing human beings bypass

Laws had been made by our dear Lord
Under His benevolent sword

NAIVE GIRL

She's naive extraordinarily
Identity is hidden completely

Trying to show her personality
To the world so full of uncertainty

Come, accept and understand me deeply
Everyone talks about me secretly

I just sit in the corner silently
Waiting for the right moment patiently

Want to say those words with humility
My heart always speaks up with honesty

And the truth shall prevail eventually
Every scar is healing gradually

HAPPY BIRTHDAY

Today's your birthday my sweet little girl
You are now sixteen, let us dance and twirl

Singing songs aloud on your special day
Enjoy with your friends, while I'm here far
away

Dream big and rise high, go and touch the sky
Let your laughter soar and craziness fly

Feel the love and care that this moment brings
Blow your candles and let your new wish
springs

Cherish the time now and save in your heart
And know that you have been loved from the
start

Narrative Poem

YOU CAME INTO MY LIFE

You came into my life when I have nothing in
it
And you make my heart skipped a beat
I knew in an instant we were destined to meet
You always showed up and I feel very sweet

As you looked at me and your eyes locked on
mine
A warm subtle chill crept up and down my
spine
Your gentle care gives my heart hope to shine
From my past heartache and now I feel fine

You asked for a house visit, I was not in the
mood
But given no choice, I waited subdued
What a surprise though when I opened the
door
So sweetly amazed, I almost fell to the floor

You walked inside the house, and the closer
you came
The warmer my skin, the warmer the flame

You give me a dozen fresh roses, asking for my
YES
I don't remember that I immediately say YES

You offered your arms and asked me to give a
hug
And I feel like there was a light from the
ladybug
That was the day that our love story began
We then enjoy each moment and so was our
plan
The two lives once spent alone then became
one
Our love like no other could never be undone.

You've kept my heart in your hands ever since
then
You proved your love to me was real again
and again
Eighteen months later we were husband and
wife
I've always thanked God that you came into
my life

Assonance Poem

I AM NOT AWARE

I have to decide life that I want for myself
The life I have to live on this planet earth
before the time I need to say goodbye
I need to get ready, pack up my belongings,
my life, my soul my body, and my bones
into a coffin while I am still breathing

On this day, I need you to slum me
with a harsh judgment informing me
that it is time to book a ticket of flight death
when you were supposed to look
and mend my broken heart
In my early life, I have to decide for myself
to catch a flight that would depart at midnight
I have to leave my dreams behind unfulfilled
when I thought I was brought
into this world with a purpose to survive

Now, I have a life full of sadness
I am not aware that I need to catch a flight
death
to heaven in my early years of existence
because of my unexplained sickness

Unexplained as I don't know how to find
the answer to why I have it
I need you my love to come and save me
Save me from everything that is happening
not even in my control
Without my understanding, I am not aware

ACCEPTANCE

Each one of us has unique abilities
Strategies and confidence of mentality
Is what we prefer in any event or games
It's either we go for the win or we lose
Acceptance is what makes us happier
Glorify and cheer if you win
Praise, sanctify your victory
Celebrate, proclaim and be happy
Take a break, appreciate and enjoy

Acknowledge it when you lose
It may be difficult, hard, and dangerous
In every battle, the downfall is inevitable
The chances of losing are always reasonable
We can never win and succeed all the time
There is a chance you will be the winner
You may also lose and fail, but it doesn't matter
The most meaningful thing is
You aspire, strive, and did your best

EMOTIONS INSIDE

Thinking of you from sunrise till night
My heart feels breaking without you in my
sight
Checking on my phone to see your messages
Not reading one I'm gonna miss you for ages
Dialed your number you were always offline
And if I won't hear your voice I'm not fine

I look for your photo that I kept in my pocket
Gives me joy and pleasure to go on my work
I'll always urge to talk with you
Because in your absence I feel out of the blue
I want to find an answer to all of my queries
Issues are all lines without an answer in series
I seek to find responses to all of my doubts
Before my mind lets out, gives you extra
shouts

Elegy Poem

A MOTHER TO ME

You became my mother as I grew up,
Lend a hand when my day was rough,
Always sat and listened to all my stupid stuff.
You helped me in any way that you could,
You always did what you said you would.
Cheering me up to make me smile,
And I knew you'd walk a mile.
To me, you were always patient and kind,
Most of the time you gave me a good peace of
mind.

The moment I knew that your gone,
My heart is torn into pieces,
For I don't know how to move on.
I cherish all the things we did together,
And I'll keep them close to my heart forever.
It's hard and not a day will go by,
That for you I will not cry.
I know your spirit's now in a better place,
As your body is in that wooden case.
After a time I will no longer mourn,
Still, my heart will be torn.

Oh my grandma, you are being loved,
And forever be missed, by me and everyone.
You were so happy and full of life,
You never seemed to have any strife.
You cared about others rather than yourself,
I'll keep our pictures by my bed on the shelf.
I am being spoiled for giving me,
Whatever I would need and desire,
You've been gladly given up your seat.
And I guess God needed you more,
no matter how much our hearts are sore.

You will never be forgotten,
you will always be in our thoughts.
Thank you for all the times we shared,
and all the times you cared,
for me and even my children.
They still remember how you cared for them.
Thank you for all the memories we made,
and all the times you paid.
I know we'll never truly part,
for this is just your new start.

I never want to say good-bye,
because that would be a lie.
For I know you'll always be with me,

even though I will not be able to truly see.
I can feel you whenever I am in weary,
You will always guide me to be in my best,
As you want me to live my life to the fullest.

193

LONGING FOR YOUR LOVE

I don't know the feeling
of having a mother by my side.
To care and to love,
to give comfort
when I needed it the most.
Sometimes I just find myself
sitting in the corner
asking why of all people on earth
you are the one who leaves
and not seeing
your daughter growing up.

Why do I need to feel
so unhappy and alone?
Why I need to experience
being criticized by my fellow kids
having no mother with me,
every birthday I have,
every school activity,
every heartache,
every time I fail,
every day in my life.

I miss you mother!
I am longing for your love.

My heart is crying now and then.
My life is incomplete.
I am still searching for that piece
that I needed to make it whole.

I needed you in my life!
I need........
-----------------you!

Twin Cinema Poem

THANK YOU
ARROGANT

I am complacent to say   how
arrogant is the person
I thank you very much   for
expressing true feelings
for always being there   even
how hurtful the words
your gentle, friendly care   the
emotions truly matters
You helped me to get fairer   I
don't like to get involved
you stopped me to feel regret   the
situation might get worst
You helped me through the hard times
think of the consequences
you stopped me to keep looking back   wake
up and move on

Simple
Emotional

I am a simple woman   I don't
understand what's going on?
not glamorous nor beautiful   I am just
simply me
not perfect   more
often weak
when I look in the mirror   with
different personality
I am a simple woman   never
expect to be high
know what I deserve   to be
loved, to be respected
I deserved to aim high   to be
prospered
I am a simple woman   I always
got emotional
never pleased anyone   doesn't
bother if you like me or not
have positive friends around   correct
every mistake
I will never change to be perfect   to
become a different person
I just want to be simple   like I
was before
Ex-Lover   Alone

My ex-lover, left me
being alone,
broken-hearted, selfless
doubt, a lonely girl.
Thank you, ex-lover,
true worth,
you define the real you!
tired to be better,
you taught me, to be braver,
myself,
you abandoned me!
challenging world.
You ruined my life!
once more!
You broke my heart!
Now, you're gone,
be unique!
I won't miss you at all!
purpose!
Thinking of you no more!
on,
I am happier,
yesterday's fall
I deserved better.
future of my own.

I ended up

without a

I realized my

I will never, get

to defend

all alone, in this

I will never fall

I will rise high!
I am worthy to

I have a

I have moved

from

for a great

Concrete Poem

Rainbow

Tremendjous rajn into our life,

Falls down from heaven's up above. Believe it is just a test,
How far we can hold our faith. The tears flowing. Freely from the eyes
Every struggle in life, Will give you more strength.
Rain turns into a storm. Takes away everything.
Emotions tore into pieces, Nothing else to reserve.
Rainbow is still somewhere. Gives a new beginning.
After each storm in life, Reminds you of hope.

You can still shine!

Time is Precious

Time is so precious,

We need to value,

Every second on it.

Giving meaning,

For everything we do.

Give the best hope;

For the future to experience.

Give the best effort,

On every

challenge we had.

Give the best memories,

On every day of our life,

Lifediary511

Love is   it brings us
Love is extraordinary, our fantasy, it express strong feelings of affection, to people you loved most, to the things you love to do. Love is giving and caring, show your kindness, your willingness, to care to others, above your own. Love is dramatic sudden feelings of attraction and respect.

Love is a fleeting and like and care. without giving trust to one another. feeling that gives you true loyalty, each and everyone, take away the hatred and give ourselves the freedom to love and be loved. Most importantly, love yourself it's all that matters.

emotion of affection Love is hard to imagine Love is a gentle Spread love to

Lifediary511

201

Simple	Emotional
I am a simple woman	I don't understand what's going on?
not glamorous nor beautiful	I am just simply me
not perfect	more often weak
when I look in the mirror	with different personality
I am a simple woman	never expect to be high
know what I deserve	to be loved, to be respected
I deserved to aim high	to be prospered
I am a simple woman	I always got emotional
never pleased anyone	doesn't bother if you like me or not
have positive friends around	correct every mistake
I will never change to be perfect	to become a different person
I just want to be simple	like I was before

Ex-Lover

My ex-lover, left me
broken-hearted, selfless
Thank you, ex-lover,
you define the real you!
you taught me, to be braver,
you abandoned me!
You ruined my life!
You broke my heart!
Now, you're gone.
I won't miss you at all!
Thinking of you no more!
I am happier,
I deserved better.

Alone

I ended up being alone,
 without a doubt, a lonely girl.
I realised my true worth.
I will never, get tired to be better,
to defend my self,
 all alone, in these challenging world.
I will never fall once more!
I will rise high!
I am worthy to be unique!
I have a purpose!
I have moved on,
from yesterday's fall
for great future of my own.

Lifediary511

I AM WORTHY

As a woman,
we need to know our worth.
We need to see
how we stand on our own.
We need to make sure,
we are not isolated.
We need to show the world,
uniqueness,
and authenticity.

I am a woman!
I am beautiful!
I trust and respect myself.
I am simple yet strong!
I've gone through hell
and kept walking.
I know my weaknesses.
I am confident!
I walked through my past
and healed into the present.
I am powerful!
I am the author of my own life.
I exert, initiate,
and moves on my own.
I am bold!

I refused to surrender
except for my truest self
and wisest voice.
I refuse to lose my faith
in the goodness of humanity.
I am imperfect!
I do have imperfections
but that doesn't make me
imperfect.
I am perfect as I am.
I am ME!
I will never be alone.
I will always be with ME.

I am a woman!
I am worthy!
Sometimes,
I need to prove my worth.
Sometimes,
others can't see
and just ignore my presence.
Sometimes,
other misjudgment makes me
feel unworthy.
As I go on to my life journey,
meet and surround me
with people who can see

my personality,
who valued my hard work,
who appreciate me
for just being me.

But sometimes,
there is always a dark side
from people, I am dealing with.
Sometimes, I failed.
Proving myself poorly,
and my worth depreciated.
Others can see me clearly
on my mistakes alone.
Ignoring my selfless care,
dedication, and commitment
to do things to their advantage.
Some never appreciate
everything I did,
rather looking for a reason
for humiliation.

As a woman,
I need to rise!
I need to learn!
Now, I am learning
the value of worth every day
with the awareness that

self-care and self-love.
I will never stop
surrounding myself
with resilient, brave,
and positive women.
I learned a lot about
my personality from everyone.
I have learned people
are naturally good,
but make bad choices
in bad circumstances sometimes.
Sharing knowledge to earn
someone's trust
and respect and gain
an extraordinary friendship
and lend a hand
without expecting anything in return.
I feed my mind
with food of positiveness.
I choose to give up
my passion
and gently terminates
the devil of negativity.

As a woman,
I need to be firm.
Not only for myself

but also for every woman,
I am talking to
and those who trusted me so.
For the young ones
who aim to know their worth.
For my daughter
who looks up to me.
I am a woman!
I am empowered!
I dedicate myself to motivate
another woman!
I commit myself to guide
women to find their inner strength
to keep moving on
to reach their goals
and be the best version
that they are aiming for.

I am a woman!
And I am proud!

THE TONGUE

I've heard a lot of words
Good and bad from others mouth
I've seen how they speak the words
Without noticing they can hurt

I've seen what words can do
To me, to you, and anyone
As I deal with people everywhere
The tongue is so powerful!
We need to control and use with care

I've seen nasty and spiteful words
That can damage and ruin one life
And gentle words that heal and bless
I've seen careless words stir up strife
And tender words ease anguish and distress

I've watched silence speak out loud
Idle and foolish rumour bring misconduct
Seen timely words persuade a crowd
And hasty and bold words end in grief

I've seen people eat their words
People can't seem to hold their tongue
I've seen them take the shame it pays for

When they are later proved wrong and untrue

My tongue, too, can go astray
Please Lord, help me watch with care
To whom I need to talk with
To what I need to say and speak
How I need to speak
When I need to speak
Where I need to talk

BOOK OF LIFE

Year's come and goes by,
just a blink of an eye.
Moments of darkness, grief, and isolation.
Pleasures and happiness flew by.
Everyone I cared for and loved
has come and has gone.
But my life journey never stopped,
I carried on with pride.
Life wasn't easy, struggles were always there.
Refreshed with the significant time.
Times I just didn't care.

I stood up on my own,
and I still found my way,
Through some nights filled with tears,
and the dawn of new days coming.
Now that my existence been so far,
it's become very clear,
things I once found important,
were not why I was in here breathing.

No matter how many things,
I managed to accomplish,
were never what made me,
feel proud and better deep inside.

Those worries and fears,
that haunted and bothered me each day,
at the end of it, all would just fade away.

No matter how much I reached out,
to other people when needed,
wouldn't be the true calculation,
of how I have been succeeded.
I dealt with my soul and my heart,
it wouldn't ultimately beset me apart.

What's powerful and important now,
is that my opinion of myself alone,
whether or not, I'm the best I can be.
And that kindness, unpretentiousness,
and love to humanity that I conveyed,
will reveal that I am blessed and honored
to live my life with grace and dignity.

Before my life will end and the Lord tells me,
it's my time to go, the book of my life story
that I loved and treasure will then be ended,
and the world will always find a way
.... to read and reminisce.

I am ready and I will always be.

ABOUT THE AUTHOR

Ailenemae Salvador Ramos is from Jones Isabela, Philippines. Happily married for 17 years and a proud mother of 16 years old young lady and a 15 years old young man.
She is presently working in Hong Kong since July 2010.
She loves reading and writing. She finds writing as an easy way to express her emotions. Scribbling what comes to her mind until she can create some ideas to form a poem. Every piece she wrote is usually based on her

own life story. She loves to share it with everyone and wishes that readers can adapt some lessons about them.

Ailenemae performed in the Carnival of Poetry; a monthly online poetry reading gathering last November 22, 2020.

Also, Ailenmae's Two poems; Paradise, (Paraiso) and Love our Nature (Mahalin ang Kalikasan) was published in The Tiger Moth Review issue #5 from Migrant Writers of Singapore last January 2021.

As of now, she's still exploring and trying to learn more things to improve herself on something she loves to do specifically in writing.

Ailenemae is a member of a positive and empowered ladies group, the "Cinderella's Angels" lead by two humble ladies in the Poetry world that guides everyone to improve their writing and teaching them to bring out the best of themselves.

As a mother, Ailenemae wants the best for her family, as she plans to go home someday, hoping that her kids will achieve their goals in life.